D0536330

Franklin and the Big Small Case

Kids Can Press

FRANKLIN and his friends liked to play detectives. Together, they searched for clues to solve mysteries. They called themselves the Super Cluepers.

One day, when they were playing in the yard, they heard Harriet yelling, "Help! Help!"

"This sounds like a job for the Super Cluepers!" said Franklin. He and his friends immediately changed into their super detective selves.

"Mega Bear is my name," said Bear. "With my cupcakes of power, I'm stronger than anybody!"

"With a voice like thunder, I'm no other than Thunder Boy!" said Snail.

"I'm Galaxy Gal, the magic girl with the magic wand!" said Goose.

"And I'm Green Wonder!" said Franklin.

"I'm Book Whiz, the smartest of the smarts!" said Beaver.

"Everyone calls me Kid Gizmo," said Fox. "I'm the greatest gadget guy in the world!"

"I'm Giggler, the funniest kid ever!" said Rabbit.

The Super Cluepers found Harriet by the house.

"Super Cluepers," said Harriet, "I can't find Lilly Kitty anywhere. Will you help me?"

"Let's Super Clueper do it!" said Green Wonder.

The Super Cluepers decided to retrace Harriet's steps.

"Harriet, where were you right before we found you?" asked Galaxy Gal.

"At a tea party," said Harriet.

"Aha!" exclaimed Giggler. "Our first clue. Let's go!"

The Super Cluepers followed Harriet to the living room.

Kid Gizmo pulled out his special X-ray scope. He looked around the room.

"This is where Harriet's tea party was," said Kid Gizmo. "But I don't see Lilly Kitty anywhere."

Thunder Boy crawled out from under a tea towel. "I found another clue!" he said. "Look over here!"

The Super Cluepers gathered around. When Green Wonder pulled the tea towel away, he found muddy footprints.

Green Wonder bent down to get a closer look. "They're just like mine, but smaller," he observed.

"Are they Harriet's?" asked Giggler.

"They're Harriet's all right," said Green Wonder. "Good clue finding, Thunder Boy. Book Whiz, write this clue down!"

Book Whiz drew the footprint in her clue book. Then she noticed something else.

"Look! There's more!" Book Whiz said, pointing to a long trail of muddy footprints.

The Super Cluepers followed the footprints outside. They led to the vegetable garden and then suddenly stopped. A hose was on the ground, and there was mud all around.

"Now I remember!" said Green Wonder. "Harriet was helping my mom pick lettuce this morning."

"Harriet must have gotten her feet dirty here and walked inside for the tea party," said Book Whiz.

"It also means she could have left Lilly Kitty somewhere near the garden," added Green Wonder.

"Let's look around," said Galaxy Gal.

The Super Cluepers searched the garden. They didn't find Lilly Kitty. But they did find a piece of paper with a drawing on it.

"What is it?" asked Mega Bear.

Kid Gizmo zoomed in with his Super Eye. "It's a gumball machine," he declared.

"Where is there a gumball machine?" asked Thunder Boy.
"There's one in front of Mr. Mole's store," said Book Whiz. "Everybody knows that!"

"Of course!" said Green Wonder. "Before gardening, Harriet and my mom went into town to run some errands."

"Maybe Harriet forgot Lilly Kitty in the village square!" said Galaxy Gal.

"This is a big clue," said Mega Bear.

"That's why it's going straight into the clue book," said Book Whiz.

"It's also why *we're* going straight to town!" exclaimed Green Wonder.

The Super Cluepers ran to Mr. Mole's store. They found the gumball machine, but not Lilly Kitty.

They looked all around the store, but they could not find her anywhere.

"She's got to be here somewhere," said Green Wonder. He thought and he thought, then he got an idea. "Book Whiz, do you still have Harriet's drawing in the clue book?"

"Yes, here it is," she said.

Green Wonder took the drawing. "If we match up Harriet's drawing with what we see in front of us, we'll know exactly where she was when she drew it!"

"There!" said Galaxy Gal. "She must have drawn it by the gazebo."

When the Super Cluepers got to the gazebo, Lilly Kitty was not there. But Mega Bear found a big hole in the floor. It was dark inside, so Kid Gizmo shone his Looking Light.

"Look!" yelled Green Wonder.

"It's Lilly Kitty," said Galaxy Gal.
"We have to get her out of there," said Book Whiz. "But how?"

"I'll save her!" said Thunder Boy. He quickly crawled inside to where
Lilly Kitty was lying.

Thunder Boy tried lifting Lilly Kitty. "She's too heavy," he said.

Green Wonder had an idea. He ran to Mr. Mole's store to borrow
an umbrella.

Then he stuck the umbrella in the hole — and pulled out Thunder Boy and Lilly Kitty!

"We solved the mystery!" said Green Wonder.

"Good work, Thunder Boy," said Giggler.

The Super Cluepers brought Lilly Kitty back to Harriet.

"Oh, thank you, Super Cluepers!" she said. "Would you like to stay for tea and some treats? I'm having a tea party."

"Don't mind if we do," said Green Wonder.

"And don't forget about Lilly Kitty," said Galaxy Gal.

"That's right," said Green Wonder. "After all, she's the guest of honor!"